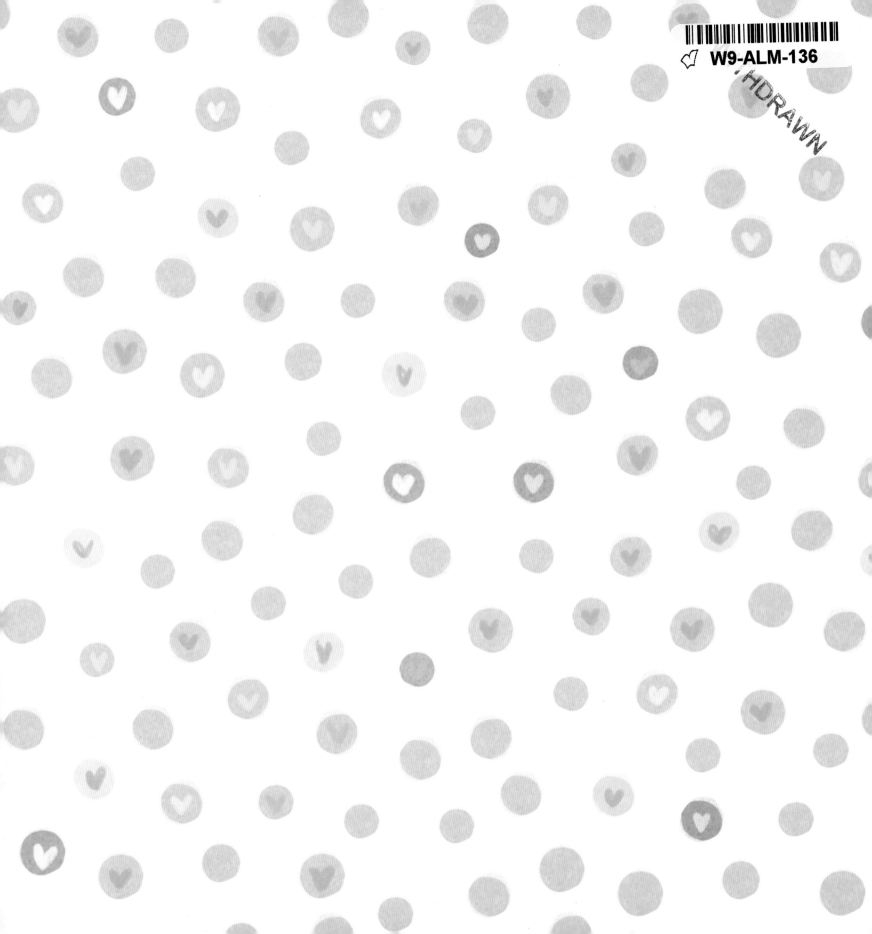

Olive

the Alien

by Katie Saunders

little bee books

Olive was Archie's baby sister. She was fluffy, frilly, very pink, and looked a bit like a marshmallow.

Archie **LOVED** Olive very much. But Archie didn't always understand his little sister. Sometimes, Olive's behavior could be very confusing.

Olive seemed to speak a language that didn't make any sense.
Mommy called it "baby talk." But Archie just thought it sounded odd.

Olive also cried a lot and could be very, VERY loud. Sometimes she cried for no reason at all!

The more Archie thought about it, the stranger Olive seemed.
Archie started to think that Olive might be an alien from

OUTER SPACE!

Olive slept a lot and could fall asleep anywhere.

She had to have her food all mashed together into teeny,
tiny pieces. Archie thought it looked DISGUSTING.
Meal times were always really messy.

"Olive has to be an alien for **SURE!**" said Archie.

Bath times were very interesting, too. Archie wondered if maybe aliens weren't allowed to get wet, because Olive screamed in the bath and splashed water everywhere.

Whenever Mommy took Olive and Archie outside for a walk,
people always made **peculiar** noises and **silly** faces at Olive.
"Aliens must have special superpowers to make normal
people act so **strange**," thought Archie.

Sometimes Mommy would hang Olive in a weird contraption she called a baby bouncer. Olive bounced for hours, laughing to herself.

Archie found this very odd indeed.

One of the strangest things about Olive was that
EVERYTHING went in her mouth.

Like **toys...**

the **cat's tail...**

socks...

and even her own TOES!

And one of the worst things about Olive was
when Mommy had to change her.
It was the most
DISGUSTING THING THAT
ARCHIE HAD EVER SMELLED!

Olive simply had to be an alien.

"Archie, Olive isn't from outer space," said Mommy.

"She's just a baby."

Archie wasn't convinced. He was SURE that Olive had come from another planet.

Then one day, Archie's big cousin, William, came over to play.

"**WOW**, Archie, you are really lucky," said William.

"I wish my little brother Ned had all these cool toys."

Archie was quite **surprised.**

But he was even more surprised when Ned sat next to Olive and started speaking to her in the same strange language!

"He always makes sounds like that," William said. "That's just what babies do."
"Really?" said Archie. "Maybe all babies speak the same language."

At play time, Olive and Ned **ate** their shoes and socks.

At dinnertime, Olive and Ned made a **mess.**

They **pulled** the cat's tail.

And they both cried really
LOUDLY!

"Maybe all babies eat **strange** things, make **huge** messes, and scream **VERY, VERY** loudly," Archie said.

"I'm sorry, Olive," said Archie. "I guess I was wrong. You're not an alien—you're just a baby." Archie gave Olive an ENORMOUS cuddle.
"I was a baby once, too. Maybe I was just as strange as you are!"

"Oh my," said Archie, holding his nose.

"Maybe I was wrong after all. The smell Olive is making is
OUT OF THIS WORLD!"

For Archie Gray and Olive Honey
love Mommy xxxx

little bee books
An imprint of Bonnier Publishing Group
853 Broadway, New York, New York 10003
Text and illustration copyright © 2015 by Katie Saunders.
First published in Australia by The Five Mile Press.
This little bee books edition, 2016.
All rights reserved, including the right of reproduction in whole
or in part in any form. LITTLE BEE BOOKS is a trademark of
Bonnier Publishing Group, and associated colophon is a trademark
of Bonnier Publishing Group.
Manufactured in China 0715 HH
First Edition 2 4 6 8 10 9 7 5 3 1
Library of Congress Cataloging-in-Publication Data
is available upon request.
ISBN 978-1-4998-0195-8

littlebeebooks.com
bonnierpublishing.com